This book belongs to:

....

SIGMUND'S BIRTHDAY SURPRISE

Written & Illustrated by John Patience

The birds were singing and the early morning sunshine was shining through the trees, as Mr. Periwinkle the Postman came driving along the lane in his mail van. Normally Mr. Periwinkle did his rounds on his bicycle, but this morning he had an especially large birthday present to deliver to Sigmund Swamp. It was a long wooden crate, and rather strange snorting noises were coming out of it! The crate was very heavy and Sigmund had to help Mr. Periwinkle carry it into the house.
"It says, 'From Uncle Oscar to Sigmund on his birthday'", said Sigmund, reading the label. "I wonder what it can be."

Carefully, Sigmund began to pry the lid off the crate.
As he did this the snorting noises from inside grew louder
and louder, until at last the lid popped open and out
crawled an enormous crocodile! In the twinkling of an
eye, Mr. Periwinkle rushed out to his van and drove
away, and Sigmund scrambled up on top of a cupboard.
Meanwhile, the crocodile began to gobble up the poor
toad's breakfast. He was very hungry. In fact, he hadn't
had a bite to eat since he left the Amazon jungle, where
Uncle Oscar had caught him!

Having polished off Sigmund's breakfast, the crocodile still felt hungry and went off looking for more. He made his way through the garden and slid into the river Ferny. As he swam past the school, the children were playing ball. Spike Willowbank gave the ball an extra hard kick which sent it flying over the playground wall. It would have landed in the river, but the crocodile caught it in his mouth and made a nice little snack of it.

When the crocodile reached
the dam at Mr. Croaker's
watermill, he climbed out of
the river and wandered around
until he came upon Mrs.
Prickles, who was hanging out
her laundry.

"Good gracious," cried Mrs. Prickles, almost jumping out of her shoes. "It's a crocodile!" And she scurried into her house and bolted the door behind her. As for the crocodile, he took a liking to the laundry and ate the sheets, pillowcases and all.

Mrs. Prickles's laundry had been very tasty, but now the crocodile sniffed the air and caught a scent that was absolutely delicious. It was coming from the bakery where Mr. Acorn had just finished baking a batch of cream buns and jam tarts. What a feast they made! The crocodile ate every last one of them, smacked his lips, and then devoured a shelf of crusty loaves.

"Go away at once," shouted Mr. Acorn, waving his rolling pin angrily. But the greedy animal didn't leave until he had eaten everything in sight.

By this time, Sigmund had informed P. C. Hoppit about the escaped crocodile, and together they set out to track him down. They hadn't been searching long when Sigmund heard an odd little sound coming from behind a tree.

"Boo-hoo. Boo-hoo-oo."

It was the crocodile and he was crying.

"Dear me," whispered P. C. Hoppit. "What can be the matter with him?"

"I expect he's feeling lonely," replied Sigmund. "After all, he is the only crocodile in Fern Hollow."

"Yes," agreed P. C. Hoppit. "I think I'd better telephone Poppletown Zoo to come and take him away. There are bound to be other crocodiles at the zoo to keep him company."

Before long, a Zookeeper arrived in a large van with a cage on the back. On the Zookeeper's instructions the cage was baited with a tray of hot swiss rolls, supplied by Mr. Acorn. Then everyone hid themselves and waited. The crocodile was still crying behind his tree, but when he

caught the delicious smell of the swiss rolls he quickly
perked up and crawled out to investigate. The moment he
was in the cage the Zookeeper leapt out from his hiding
place and locked the door.

"Hooray!" cried everyone.

"Mmmm," said the crocodile, munching the swiss rolls.

It turned out that Sigmund's Uncle Oscar had intended
to send the crocodile to the zoo. Instead he had
sent them a crate of Amazon honey, which was really
Sigmund's birthday present. He had simply mixed up
the labels. The crocodile settled in nicely at the zoo,
where Sigmund visited him from time to time and fed
him a few of Mr. Acorn's cream buns!